A panther sees a fox.
Yum!

“Stop,” yells the fox. “I am King of this forest!”

"We shall see," thinks the panther.

The bats flap off.

The frogs jump into the pond.

The pangolin coils up.

The lizard runs under a log.

"He is indeed King of this forest," thinks the panther as he runs off.

Teachers and parents

An important part of becoming a confident, fluent reader is a student's ability to understand what they are reading. Below are some suggestions on how to develop a student's reading comprehension. Make reading this book a shared experience between you and the student. Try to avoid leaving it until the whole book is read before talking about it. Occasionally stop at various intervals throughout the book.

- Ask questions about the characters, the setting, and the meaning;
- Encourage the student to think about what might happen next. It does not matter if the answer is right or wrong, so long as the suggestion makes sense and demonstrates understanding;
- Relate what is happening in the book to any real-life experiences the student may have;
- Pick out any vocabulary that may be new to the student and ask what they think it means. If they don't know, explain it and relate it to what is happening in the book;
- Encourage the student to summarize, in their own words, what they have read.

About this folktale

Fox Tricks Panther is based on a Chinese folktale called The Fox that Borrows the Tiger's Terror. The original version of the story features a tiger, but we have chosen to use a panther in this book because it is an easier word for the students to read.

What's in the book?

- Who says that he is King of the forest?
- Who coils up?
- Who hides under a log?

What do you think?

- Does the panther want to eat the fox?
- Is the fox really King of the forest?

Folktales

Jolly Phonics Readers are fully decodable books for new readers.

These Readers have been written with a **carefully controlled vocabulary**, and are specifically designed for students who are learning to read and write with Jolly Phonics.

- The text in these Red Level Books (first level) uses only **decodable regular words** (words that are made up from the 42 letter sounds taught in the first stage of Jolly Phonics) and a small number of **tricky words** (frequently used words that are not fully decodable at this stage).
- All of the tricky words and letter sounds used in this book are shown on the front inside cover. These can be used as a quick practice activity before starting the book.
- **Faint type** is used for silent letters, like the <b> in *lamb*.
- **Comprehension questions** and discussion topics are included at the end of the book. These ensure that students are not only able to read the text, but also get meaning from it.

Red Level Readers

Level 0 | Level 1 | Level 2 | Level 3 | Level 4 | Level 5

Folktales

The Cap Seller
Rock Broth
Fox Tricks Panther
The Cat and the Rooster
The Moon on the Millpond
The King's Cheese

MIX
Paper | Supporting responsible forestry
FSC® C016973

 Written by Emily Guille-Marrett

82 Winter Sport Lane, Williston, VT 05495, USA. Tel: +1-800-488-2665
77 Hornbeam Road, Buckhurst Hill, Essex, IG9 6JX, UK. Tel: +44 20 8501 0405

Printed in China.

www.jollylearning.com info@jollylearning.co.uk

ISBN 978-1-83582-141-1

Reference: JL1411
American English Edition